This igloo book belongs to:

Helena

igloobooks

*Designed by Laura Chamberlain*
*Edited by Daisy Edwards*

*"Unicorn Wishes" written by Stephanie Moss and illustrated by Emanuela Mannello*
*"Fairy Sprinkle's Magic Wand" written by Melanie Joyce and illustrated by Nicola Anderson*
*"Dragon to the Rescue" written by Stephanie Moss and illustrated by Jo Byatt*
*"The Magical Toy Box" written by Melanie Joyce and illustrated by James Newman Gray*

*Copyright © 2020 Igloo Books Ltd*

*An imprint of Igloo Books Group,*
*part of Bonnier Books UK*
*bonnierbooks.co.uk*

*Published in 2020*
*by Igloo Books Ltd, Cottage Farm*
*Sywell, NN6 0BJ*

*Manufactured in China. 0720 001*
*10 9 8 7 6 5 4 3 2 1*

*Library of Congress Cataloging-in-Publication*
*Data is available upon request.*

*ISBN 978-1-83852-597-2*
*IglooBooks.com*
*bonnierbooks.co.uk*

MY FIRST
Treasury
— Of —
MAGICAL
STORIES

igloobooks

# Unicorn Wishes

Eva just loved unicorns. She thought about them all day long.
If anyone said they weren't real, she was sure that they were wrong.

Unicorn toys in her bedroom were in piles ten feet high.

And she longed to see one flying gracefully up in the sky.

Eva had a pretty pony that she played with every day.
She'd pretend she was a unicorn. "Fly, Sparkle, fly," she'd say.

"But unicorns don't exist," all Eva's friends giggled with glee.

"Come to my special party," she said. "Just you wait and see!"

The stables were all decorated in pink, purple, and green.
It was the most enchanting party that Eva had ever seen!

Before her friends arrived,
Eva kissed Sparkle's soft,
warm head.

"I wish you REALLY
were a unicorn,"
she closed her eyes and said.

Then all of a sudden,
her pony began to glow.
Wings and a horn
appeared, and rainbow
hair started to grow!

8

The stunning unicorn
was far beyond her
wildest dreams.
She twinkled like the
stars and looked as
pretty as moonbeams.

Sparkle's voice was soft and gentle.
She said, "Let's fly off on the breeze!"
Eva climbed up on her back, as she cried,
"WOO-HOO! WHEE! Yes, please!"

"Your magic kiss transformed me," explained Sparkle, as they flew. "Most people don't believe in us. Most people aren't like you."

They glided past a rainbow on marshmallow clouds of white.
Then far off in the distance, something gleamed in the sunlight.

Eva saw a magic palace and,
as she looked all around,
Sparkle shook her mane and smiled,
landing gently on the ground.

The other unicorns were playing at the forest waterfall.
Eva thought they were so beautiful she had to meet them all!

"I'm Shimmer,"
said one unicorn.
"I'm Moonshine,"
said one more.

Their beauty was like nothing she had ever seen before.

To celebrate her visit, they brought her treats of every kind.
There were so many things to choose from, but Eva didn't mind!

"I hope my party is this good," she said.
"We'd all have so much fun."
With just one swish of Sparkle's tail,
Eva's special wish was done.

When it was time to go, Sparkle flew Eva through the stars. "What a magical adventure," said Eva, "and it's all ours."

18

Back home, she kissed Sparkle and said, "Thank you," in her ear.

Sparkle turned back into a pony, then Eva saw her friends appear.

"You were right all along," they said.
"This party is the best. If only unicorns were real.
Then we'd really be impressed!"

20

Eva gave a secret smile and she winked at Sparkle, too.
"You just have to believe," she said.
"Then your wish will come true."

# Fairy Sprinkle's Magic Wand

In Fairyland, the little fairies are getting their first wands.
"Here is yours, Fairy Sprinkle," says the fairy queen,
holding out a wand. "Use it once to see if it works.
Then, you must go to enchantment classes
and learn how to use it properly."
"Thank you," says Sprinkle, taking
her sparkling wand.

Fairy Redwing swishes her wand. "It works!" she cries.

PING!

Magic sparkles twinkle and twirl. Fairy Flutter changes a mushroom into a flower.

ZAP!

Fairy Lily can't quite get the hang of her wand.

PPFFEFFFF

27

When the fairy queen leaves, Sprinkle waves her wand.
Four mushrooms sparkle and change into bright flowers.
"This is fun!" cries Sprinkle. "I want to do more magic."
"No, you mustn't," says Lulabell, but Sprinkle isn't listening.

Suddenly, Fairy Candycup flutters by. She's very upset.
"I want to make cupcakes for the fairy queen," she says,
trying not to cry, "but my flour bag has a hole in it.
I can't make my superspecial cupcakes without flour."

"Yes, you can!" cries Sprinkle, giggling.
Sprinkle lifts her wand and waves it
delicately over a patch of little flowers.
Magic sparkles twinkle and twirl.

ZZZZING!

In a flash, the flowers turn into cupcakes with yummy pink frosting on the top. "That was amazing, Sprinkle!" cries Candycup, fluttering her wings and smiling. "I shall tell all my friends how clever you are."

Soon, there is a line of little fairies waiting to see Sprinkle. Fairy Flutter wants to fix her torn dress.

ZING!

Fairy Bo wants long, golden hair.

PING!

"Please can I have a bowl of fairy chocolates, Sprinkle?" asks Fairy Lily. "Of course you can," says Sprinkle, swishing her wand daintily.

31

The fairies think Sprinkle is very smart to do
magic without going to enchantment classes.
"My magic is brilliant," says Sprinkle, smiling.
The more sparkling magic Sprinkle does,
the more all the other little fairies want.

"I want a pair of red shoes," says Fairy Bluebell.

PING!

"I want a pet rabbit," says Fairy Flora.

ZING!

"I want a pretty new dress," says Fairy Honeywing. Soon, Sprinkle is the most popular fairy in Fairyland.

POP!

33

"My magic is fantastic!" says Sprinkle, giggling.
"I can do anything I want to, whenever I want to."
Lulabell is fed up with Sprinkle boasting about her magic.

"I bet you can't make the stars fall from the sky and put them in this jar," says Lulabell. "I bet I can," says Sprinkle, holding up her wand.

ZZZING!

Sprinkle holds the jar and raises her wand, saying the magic words. "Stars so twinkly, stars so bright, fly to me this moonlit night."

One by one, the stars start to fall gently from the sky.

Then, the stars fall faster and faster until they are whizzing around like little fireworks. "Watch out!" cry the fairies, ducking out of the way.

Sprinkle holds up the glass jar for the stars to fly into, but they just whiz past it. "Do something, Sprinkle!" cry the fairies.

"Stars, fly into this jar!" shouts Sprinkle.
The stars just whiz faster than before, around
and around, making everyone feel quite dizzy.

Then, all of Sprinkle's spells start to go wrong.
"My cupcakes are getting bigger and bigger," says Candycup.
"My hair just won't stop growing!" cries Fairy Bo.
"My bunny rabbit is getting fatter," says Fairy Flora.
"My chocolates have grown into a mountain!" cries Fairy Lily.

Sprinkle tries and tries to stop the spells, but nothing seems to work. "Oh, no, what have I done?" she says, beginning to cry. The other little fairies put their arms around Sprinkle.

40

"Don't cry, Fairy Sprinkle," they say. "It will be all right."
"I should have gone to enchantment classes," says Sprinkle.
"I've made a mess of everything. The fairy queen will be so angry." 41

Suddenly, the fairy queen appears. She looks at the whizzing stars and the other strange things that Sprinkle's magic has done. "Oh, dear," she says. "What has happened here?"

ZZZAPPP!

"It's my fault, Fairy Queen," says Sprinkle with a little sob.
The fairy queen smiles. "Never mind," she says, gently.
"A little bit of magic will soon put things right."
The fairy queen waves her wand and says some secret words.

The stars fly up to the sky and settle in their proper places.
The cupcakes shrink, the chocolate mountain
disappears, and soon, everything is right again.
"Thank you," says Sprinkle, smiling.

44

"It was brave of you to admit your mistake, Sprinkle," says the fairy queen. "Now, off to bed, fairies. Tomorrow, you will begin enchantment classes."
"I can't wait!" says Sprinkle, and everyone laughs. With that, the little fairies flutter off to bed knowing that everything is just as it should be in Fairyland.

# Dragon to the Rescue

Albert was new at school and he felt quite nervous and shy.
He watched the other dragons **loop-the-loop** around the sky.

**Whoosh!**

went the scorching flames. . .

. . . as fire **swirled** around the air.

Albert was so amazed that he stopped to look and stare.

FIRE SAFETY

When Albert asked to have a go, he learned the teacher's special rule.

**"To make sure that you're safe, you must only breathe fire at school!"**

52

Albert understood, but his classmates whispered together...

... "Those school rules are silly. We should forget them forever!"

In the next day's fire class, everyone performed like a pro.
Albert started to feel nervous as he waited to go.

54

Albert **spluttered...**

...and **coughed.**

Then he let out a...

...**loud croak!**

But instead of flames of fire, he coughed up little puffs of smoke!

Albert felt confused. He took one more deep breath and blew.
He closed his eyes, but this time, he **sneezed** a smoky. . .

"**He can't do it,**" said the dragons.
"**He shouldn't be here!**" they cried.

So, poor Albert flew away from school, to find somewhere to hide.

Albert came across a waterfall where he could sit and think.
His throat felt so dry from coughing that he had a long, cool drink.

He took **gulp** after **gulp**, until his cheeks bulged large and round.

But suddenly, Albert paused when he heard a familiar sound.

There were flames going **whoosh** as the naughty dragons flew about.

60 Albert was so surprised, he couldn't help **spitting** his water out!

His classmates couldn't believe it. They watched their flames all disappear.

"What are you doing?" cried Albert. "You know you can't breathe fire here!"

Albert felt so **angry.** He shouted **louder** than ever before. Suddenly, before he knew it, he let out a great big, **fiery...**

ROAR

RR!

"I can breathe fire after all!" cried Albert. "My throat is cured," he said.

"But I like being different. I want to be a firefighter instead!"

Albert **zoomed** back to school, but then suddenly he froze.
Before he arrived, a smoky smell went up his nose!

**"We kept on breathing fire,"** one of the naughty dragons cried.

**"But we couldn't put it out, no matter how hard we all tried."**

**"I know how to help,"** said Albert. **"Don't worry, everyone."**

He took a gulp of water...

...then with a **hiss,** the flames were gone.

"Thank you!" they all cried. "You're the bravest dragon in the land! We always thought the rules were silly, but now we understand."

The next day at school, Albert arrived to **claps** and **cheers.**
Now he'd found his talent, he forgot all of his fears.

Well Done, Albert!

Suddenly he was a hero and his teacher thought so, too.
Now when he grew up, Albert knew just what he would do.

69

# The Magical
# Toy Box

The clock struck twelve at Lucy's house and she was fast asleep.
Across the moonlit bedroom floor, shadows began to creep.

74

A sound came from the toy box. The lid creaked and opened wide.
"It's time to play," whispered Teddy, to all the toys inside.

75

Lucy was cuddled up in bed,
as snuggly as could be.
So, the toys climbed from the toy box
and shouted out, "Yippee!"

"Shh, now, don't wake Lucy.
Be quiet, you naughty toys.
Bring the disco ball," said Teddy.
"Don't make too much noise."

"Woof-woof," said Puppy, wagging his tail,
sniffing under the bed.
He pulled out the lid of an old board game.
"I've got an idea," he said.

The toys crept into the hall,
so quietly, on tiptoe.
They climbed on board
and Puppy said,

"Hold on tight.
Let's go!"

Whoo

80

oosh!

They slid down the stairs,
with a bumpety-bump.
Everyone landed,
thumpety-thump.

Creeeak!

Teddy opened the living room door.
"Come on," he said. "Let's go.
I've found the perfect place
for a brilliant toy disco."

Soon, the disco ball was glittering.
It swirled and whirled around.

"Everybody dance!" cried Teddy.
"Dig that disco sound!"

Hippo wiggled and Monkey giggled,
as all the toys began to bop.

Singing along, as he danced to the song,
Bunny went hippety-hop!

83

"Time for a break!" cried Teddy,
as his hungry tummy rumbled.
Into the kitchen, to find some food,
the happy toys all tumbled.

They piled their plates with cookies and cake
and tasty things to eat.

Monkey munched, Croc went crunch
and they gobbled up every treat.

At last the toys were really full
and couldn't eat one bite more.
It was time to tidy up,
so Bunny swept the floor.

Teddy washed the dishes
with a scrub, scrub, scrub.
Puppy dried them off
with a rub, dub, dub.

87

Outside, the stars were fading
fast and it was nearly dawn.
"Back to the toy box everyone,"
said Teddy, with a yawn.

Up the stairs, the toys all climbed,
as quickly as they could go.
Teddy felt very sleepy,
his little legs started to slow.

"Hurry," whispered Bunny,
as he hopped up into the chest.

90

"Hey! Wait for me!" cried Teddy,
who had stopped to take a rest.

The toy box lid was closing,
so Teddy laid on the floor.
Soon, he was in a deep sleep
and softly began to snore.

When she woke up in the morning, Lucy stretched
and rubbed her eyes. "How did my bear get over
there?" she thought, to her surprise.

92

"Lovely Bear," said Lucy, as she blinked in the
morning light, "I wonder what you were
doing, while I was asleep last night."

93